THE
LOVE STORY
OF THE
CENTURY

Märta Tikkanen

Translated by Stina Katchadourian

DEEP VELLUM PUBLISHING
DALLAS, TEXAS

Deep Vellum Publishing
3000 Commerce St., Dallas, Texas 75226
deepvellum.org · @deepvellum

Deep Vellum is a 501c3 nonprofit literary arts organization
founded in 2013 with the mission to bring
the world into conversation through literature.

Copyright © Märta Tikkanen, 1978
Original version published in Swedish as *Århundradets kärlekssaga*
Published by agreement with Helsinki Literary Agency (Helsinki, Finland)
Original translation copyright © Stina Katchadourian, 1984
Revised translation copyright © Stina Katchadourian, 2020
First Deep Vellum edition, 2020

A version of this translation was published by
Rhodora Books/Capra Press in 1984

Support for this publication has been provided in part by grants from the National
Endowment for the Arts, the Texas Commission on the Arts, the City of Dallas
Office of Arts and Culture's ArtsActivate program, and the Moody Fund for the Arts:

ISBN: 978-1-941920-93-0 (paperback) | 978-1-941920-94-7 (ebook)

LIBRARY OF CONGRESS CATALOGING-IN-PUBLICATION DATA

Names: Tikkanen, Märta, author. | Katchadourian, Stina, translator.
Title: The love story of the century / Märta Tikkanen ; translated by
  Stina Katchadourian.
Other titles: Århundradets kärlekssaga. English
Description: First edition. | Dallas, Texas : Deep Vellum Publishing, 2020.
  | Translation of: Århundradets kärlekssaga. | Translated from the Swedish.
Identifiers: LCCN 2019038728 (print) | LCCN 2019038729 (ebook) | ISBN
  9781941920930 (trade paperback) | ISBN 9781941920947 (ebook)
Classification: LCC PT9876.3.I4 A6213 2020 (print) | LCC PT9876.3.I4
  (ebook) | DDC 839.73/74--dc23
LC record available at https://lccn.loc.gov/2019038728
LC ebook record available at https://lccn.loc.gov/2019038729

Cover Design by Anna Zylicz | annazylicz.com
Typesetting & Layout by Kirby Gann

Text set in Bembo, a typeface modeled on typefaces cut by Francesco Griffo
for Aldo Manuzio's printing of *De Aetna* in 1495 in Venice

Printed in the United States of America on acid-free paper

THE LOVE STORY
OF THE CENTURY

For Henrik

1

—

At first it feels good
incredibly and tremendously good
that in spite of everything
there are also people who see
behind the façade
who know
and realize

But then everything
only gets harder

So the question comes:
Why don't you leave?

Countless times I've been
on my way

if this drinking bout isn't
the last
I'll leave

if his malice

affects the children
I'll leave

if he also starts
to lie
I'll leave

and if he ever uses force
on me
I'll leave

when the children can no longer
take it
I'll simply have to

And it all happened
But I still didn't leave

Why?

❖

I woke you up once
in the middle of the night
and asked you
to hold me
didn't dare anymore

to trust myself

Try to sleep now
you said and turned
away

I woke you up once more
I didn't dare not to
You sat up
and looked at me
then you disappeared
into the living room's whitish gray dawn

You had a glass of whiskey
half emptied
in your hand
when you returned

God damn it
Why can't I ever be weak
you said

Then you emptied your glass
Then you lay down
Then you slept

About the way the dawn

turns into morning
there is nothing
to say

About you and me
There really isn't
much more to say
either

✦

Right in the center of a low-pressure zone
long spells of rain on all sides
storm clouds pile up beyond the forest
rain waits to pour down

Just as in the middle of a drinking bout
long wet days on every side
so far, you can sleep once you've dozed off

Never is our house so quiet

✦

An alcoholic's wife
is someone
who is always wrong

whichever way she turns

If she understands and understands
and forgives
and smoothes things out
and keeps the relatives at bay
and quiets the children
and admires
and comforts
and believes and believes and believes
and hopes

then she is a self-righteous bitch
who's always so goddamn perfect
and wonderful
an almighty one
who thinks she can move mountains
and offer forgiveness for every sin
good grief
you could vomit
when you see her shining face

And if she asks and pleads
and hides bottles
and pours out half through the window
and into the flower pots
and refuses to lie to the relatives

and blame it on the stomach flu once again
for the colleagues
and turns a deaf ear
to the five hundred and ninetieth round
of the unhappy childhood
and the unforgettable war
and the jealous colleagues

then she's a dangerous one
scheming and vindictive
and I'll be damned
if it isn't she
when it comes right down to it
who gets all those conspiracies
going everywhere
and the slander and the mudslinging campaigns

She, of course
is behind everything
who else knows so well
all those details that get thrown
into your face
she's the one sitting there like the spider in the web
all puffed up with spite, jeez

And if she finally realizes
that she has her own life

to live
and that, anyway, she can't ever live
someone else's
and not carry someone else's burdens
even if she wanted to
so very much

then she's a callous bitch
a goddamn careerist
who gets herself involved in everything
and with anyone
only just not with the person who's closest to her
and needs her the most
and who she has promised, furthermore
to love for better for worse
now we're all through with the better
as soon as things get a little worse
now she's all over the place
and dedicates herself to all kinds of nonsense
and mostly to herself
and her own success
whatever that might be, hell
but somebody else has to pay the price
remember that
although she probably won't give a damn
the goddamn bitch

And if she finally gives up
and stands there alone
with her torn nerves
and the children's torn nerves
and a thousand pangs of conscience
because she loved too little
or even loved too much,
because she did this and not that
which might have saved everything,
if she had been human enough
to understand a little better

then you can bet your life
that soon she'll have found
the next man
to sink her claws into
and torture and torment
and domineer
and play guardian angel to
until nothing else remains
for that poor devil either
but the bottle . . .

❖

I'm reading my notes
from nine books

on alcoholism

I recognize everything
I know
that the person who's grown up without love
doesn't think
that love exists

I know all the tricks
needed to satisfy
insatiable demands
more and more and more
it's never enough

I gradually get to know
the rules of the game
only too well
now coddled
now bawled out
feeling guilty about everything
and nothing
and above all about the drinking
the glory of the hangover
that finally provides punishment, longed for
and staged

I'm reading my notes

about controlling wives
of alcoholics
who must have a weak man
to keep down
and to hate through the kids
so she herself won't break down
and I read about how the wife
ingeniously seeks to thwart
all improvement

I get extremely tired

Why is it
that I'm holding on
if, in addition,
I'm the one
who sits here
and prevents you
from becoming
human?

❖

Such an honest account
of alcoholism
say the wise men in the book review sections

How come none of them
misses
the smells,
for instance?

The sharp penetrating smell of cognac
that stabs you in the gut
as soon as you come through the door
The lukewarm bulging stench
of brandy diluted by gastric juices
when you've vomited it all up

Rough redwineink
sour whitewinebelch
sweet sherry slush
gooey vermouth

But most disgusting of all
the smell of putrid hops
you breathe over me
when for the five thousandth time
you think beer enhances your sexual potency, hah!
The smell of rancid dregs hovering above everything
in the bedroom
after you've passed out with your clothes on
across our bed
the saliva

that beer brown runs down your chin
The diarrhea that follows
without fail
can be felt in the house for several days
along with that drastic purge
which makes your teeth so white

Just that
Just the smells

❖

Of course it hasn't escaped me
that there is
a rather nasty
aspect
to this thing:

Now you're lying there
blabbering
with your clothes on
unless I take them off
Now I can use
any tone of voice I prefer
when I prevent
those who call you
from speaking to you

Now you can't reach me
with some nasty sarcasm
that drives me to despair
even when you're
being unfair
because of course I know
why you're saying it—

you're scared
of me!

Now you know
that if you're going to make it
through this
one more time
it'll depend on
my giving you
the medications
exactly when you need them
and my not giving you
more booze
just when you claim
you simply can't
do without it
and my seeing to it that
you take in
salt and proteins

when your electrolyte balance is disturbed
and my calling an ambulance
and not letting you
have your way
when you refuse to lie down on the stretcher
despite the fact that you just asked
to be admitted to the hospital

and my sitting there, then
holding your hand
just when I really don't want
to hold your hand
or even see
you at all

Somehow
it's quite awful
all of this—

having the upper hand
the power
and being quite pleased
about that

Most awful to realize
that both of us
know it

❖

Somehow
it's quite awful
all of this—

having the upper hand
the power
and being quite pleased
about that

Most awful to realize
that both of us
know it

❖

For many years
you held my feet to the fire
by always talking about suicide
as soon as you drank

I kept hiding
scissors knives
jump ropes medicines
cartridges for the rifle
the clip for the revolver

threw the fishing spear
out the window
one night
when I saw how your eyes
were glued to it
black against the white
wall

Every evening
the rifle above the door
was the last thing I saw
before falling asleep
Every morning I opened my eyes
and saw the rifle
first

and I was always
grateful
that yet another day
or a night
had passed
and you were still alive

For a long time I played along
in the game you wanted
to play
with me as your partner

and your life
and my despair
at stake

Until I realized:
I can't do anything
to prevent you
if you
really want to die
The responsibility
for your life
is not mine

But I am responsible
for my life
and for the children's
and I can't live
if all my
strength
is used up
to maintain you
in a life
that you don't care about

Now I no longer see
the rifle
though I suppose

it still hangs
in its place

and you've stopped
talking about
your suicide
when you
drink

❖

Trust people
You can always trust them
to wish you well
and be decent to you
if you are decent
to them

       I am so scared
       I'm so scared that if you only knew
       how scared I am
       you wouldn't dare to live
       either

No need to be scared
Just trust people
just believe they're good

and wish each other well

>Dad was sitting with the gun
>one whole night
>he was sitting with the gun
>he said he'd shoot
>and my little brother and I
>had to sit there
>all night when you were in town
>We held each other's hands
>we were shivering
>all night

>Not even after he'd passed out
>with the rifle in his hand
>did we dare to get up and call you
>what if
>he'd woken up

>You have no idea
>how scared I am
>I'm so scared that I don't know
>if I dare to live

But I
must dare to believe
even more

Now I must believe so much
that we all
will dare to live
anyway

❖

When he is ten
he cleans and vacuums
every square inch
arranges his plastic soldiers
so all the rifles point
toward a mutual enemy
who'll be destroyed

He draws only monsters
terrifying beasts
with fifteen claws and fangs
and enormous jaws
they charge out of the pictures
and attack
everybody and everything
they're horrible and ghastly
they're crying out in terror

At night he can't get to sleep
because he's got to intervene

in case there's a fight again
then he'll divert their attention
from what they're fighting about
so their irritation
turns against him

as long as both of them are mad at him
they at least
agree
for once

At night he must sneak up and
check
that neither one has moved away
and disappeared
He pokes them just in case
so he'll know
that both of them lie there
and sleep side by side in their bed

He is always anxious
he always fears the catastrophe
he knows it's coming
only he doesn't know when
He doesn't dare
pass an open window
or cross the square

He no longer dares to go to school

soon he'll no longer
dare to go on living

♦

The day disaster is upon us again
he's the most resourceful one
and the most patient
for hours he lies close by on the bed
stroking hair from forehead
listening, talking
comforting
holding and hugging
He is right there
and never tires

Now I don't have to worry anymore
he says
because now it's happened

He grows a few years
and many inches
gets more broad-shouldered
by the day
Soon his strength

will have caught up
with the responsibility
he has carried
for so long

❖

You're talking about
how you fell asleep by the door
so many nights resting your head on your dog
how you biked around and cried
when your dog died
that the dog meant more
to you
than your father and your mother
who were never sober or home
and who didn't know
what they wanted you for

It's sad
and you cry

I'm sitting in the chair across from you
and I've got time to think a lot
because the story isn't short
and it isn't the first time
I'm hearing it

You're talking
and I sit and wonder
why you don't say anything
about the nights when your kids
haven't dared to go to sleep
but have sneaked around the corners
and spied on you—
Dad hasn't started drinking again, has he?
how's Dad?
no brandy smell
is there?
Are you really sure he won't be drinking
tonight?

While you're crying yourself to sleep
because you feel sorry for yourself
with your father who was
an alcoholic

I sit wondering when
my hatred
will burn you
to white ashes

while you're lying there, sobbing
without thinking for one second
that your kids, too, have
a father

At one time
I was hiding bottles
and quickly emptied
leftover drops
into flower pots and ashtrays
and out the window
as soon as you turned your back

Nowadays I don't give a damn
The quicker you pour the stuff into yourself
the sooner you'll pass out
and the sooner I'll be able to continue with
the things I'd rather be doing
than sitting and listening to your monologues
read to the kids
read a bit myself
or quite simply sleep
by myself

Besides, it isn't necessary
to wait long anymore
since you get drunk
on just a few drops
and vomit right away
and pass out

Practical
Saves both time
and money

❖

Earlier
you were nasty and sarcastic
only when you drank

Nowadays you're
even nastier and more sarcastic
when you're sober

One would think that you wouldn't
need to drink
now that you can be nasty anyway

But maybe it's just as well
that you drink
now and then
that way, at least you pass out
sometimes

❖

She crawls into my lap

smelling of sleep
downy baby hair on her neck
words stumble eagerly:

Guess what
I had such a strange dream last night
I dreamt that I was drinking for a whole week
and I drank and drank
and got all dizzy
but then I went to the doctor
and then I went home to my house
and then I drank for another whole week
and then I got dizzy again

Guess what
then I suddenly noticed
that I'd turned into a wolf
I was ferocious and wild and crazy
I only wanted to fight
but then my wolf daddy was coming
and we rolled in the grass
and were biting each other
but then I bit him to death you know
and then I stopped fighting right away

At the breakfast table
she tells her dream again

to everybody
all the way to the wolf daddy, there she stops abruptly
quickly smiles at me from the corner of her eye

and that was it, she says
continues to nibble
her Rice Krispies

❖

Kids
can't stand to wait
when they've got something to say
they must immediately interrupt
and get to tell
In our family
the kids must wait all through dinner
while you're expounding your thoughts
and turning your experiences inside out

Kids
can't deal with uncertainty
they want an answer
that sticks, something
they can trust
In our family
the kids must be content and accept

that you can't possibly be tied down
you must always have your freedom
to come and go whenever and wherever you choose

Kids
don't hide their jealousy
they pinch their siblings, take their
toys, tell on each other

In our family
kids have had to put up with
you tearing a favorite book apart
slandering their friends
and mocking the socialism they believe in

Kids
don't stop arguing
no matter of how often they hear
that the one who gives in is the wiser
In our family
the kids have learned early on
to avoid, they answer
Uh-uh and Oh well and Maybe you're right
and let you go on until you're tired

Kids
are not usually the ones

who feel responsible when something happens
In our family
the seven-year-old took the bottle of red wine
and hid it from the cop, half-emptied, behind his back
once when you were drunk at the wheel

Kids
don't normally protect
they are the protected ones
as long as they are helpless and small
In our family
the kids are the ones
who protect and comfort you
when you're racked by fears
and need others to shore you up

Kids
should gradually grow
into the adult world
learn to give and take
and experience but master fear
In our family
everything was there in excess from the start
but their tenderness grew all the more
for you, the child
so early given them

❖

I called up
a psychiatrist
to hear if any help was available
for me and the children
so we could solve our own problems
before it was too late
even for us

The psychiatrist, concerned, was leafing
through the listings of his brotherhood
and announced
that he had found two
who would be pretty good

The best one, he said,
I recommend we save
for your husband
in case he ever
wants help

But here, he said kindly, is the address
of the next best
for you and the children

❖

For some time now I've known how I'll react
and perhaps I can even manage
to figure out the process—
but to stop reacting
—that I somehow don't seem able to do

It begins the second or third day
of your hangover
when you're starting to realize
who you are
and where you are
and that you have a family
that's been tiptoeing around you
like ghosts
or accusations
or distorted monsters
while you were drinking

At that point you think
it's time
to take everyone to task
Then you demand
blind discipline at the table
and the pillows of the sofa must be straight
and I get
a round of abuse
because nothing works

in our house
and because quite clearly
I can't handle the children
at all, what will become of them
with such laxity
and obviously it's only you
who does any cleaning at all
in this house

That's when I feel
the explosion coming
I guess I can still
take your remarks
about the cleaning
ok, it isn't perfect
but then
there have sort of been other things
to think about the last few days
and if there's been a moment left over
it's made more sense
to try to steal
a bit of sleep
but never mind although I mutter in anger
that during the last twenty years
I actually have never seen you
touch a vacuum cleaner
ok anyway about the cleaning

But when the kids
get roughed up
if one of them happens to forget
that it's impolite to reach
at the table
or serve himself before you
when they are told
that they are impossible, horrible,
and spoiled
and should be ashamed
and sent from the table
and that you won't have anything to do with them
as ill-bred
and degenerate as they are

then my patience runs out

and then I let it spill out
it's really the limit
to strike out at them
when they've been putting up with everything
everything
for about ten days
and have helped and comforted
and held you
and been
deeply unhappy

for your sake
and now it is they
who have to suffer the consequences
of your violent guilt
and you need to put some order
in your life
SHAME ON YOU

And all this anger
that I can't heap on you
straight and unpadded
now that you're struggling anyway
to face the world
and when the worst is finally over
and you are on your way back
to life
all that anger
will have to take a detour
but you're the one it's aimed at
and it surges over you
and I truly hope
that it will drown you forever
AMEN

❖

Have you calculated

that the only thing that will force me to use
whatever remains
of my strength
is the final proof
of your weakness?

How can you trust
that there is still
anything left
of my strength?

Or is it true
that the only thing
you really can't deal with
is knowing
that even my strength
has a limit?

❖

You must be strong
people
sometimes
tell me

And I think about
all that's happened

—maybe
I'm strong

Yes, I guess that's it
I suppose I'm strong

Strong people don't bend

They break

❖

There was a letter:

I assume
that you'll survive
in spite of everything

that was enough

❖

You work methodically
and finish your jobs
for the two weeks ahead
and set up only unimportant meetings
that you've never thought of going to

you calmly lay away a supply
of everything that you might need
in order for the binge to proceed
pleasantly
and according to plan

You get cognac
a superior kind for the start
and then an inferior one, cheaper,
an emergency ration of beer
and light beer from the supermarket
and finally you ask me
to renew your prescription
of that drastic purge and your sleeping pills

Then suddenly you find yourself
with a glass in your hand
voicing your surprise
over your metabolism
that demands you start drinking
on this ordinary weekday morning
completely out of the blue

You who are such a bohemian
and absolutely can't remember
a phone number,
you never miss one single detail

when you are preparing
for your unexpected
drinking bouts

❖

For a long time I used to
correct
your slips of the tongue
and laugh about the fact
that there were words
you never seemed to learn

"Abtruptly" you say
but that just sounds funny
and "retroseptive"
but that's such an unusual word
it doesn't really matter

But when you say
"my misperception of the world"
instead of "my perception"
I prick up my ears
Never have I heard a better
or a more apt description
of the reality that surrounds you

Then I no longer dare
to correct you
How will I know
if you can stand
to see the world
without the misperceptions
you've gotten used to?

❖

In the early stage of your boozing
you suddenly see
the connections
That's when you say things
that are so breathtaking
that they are almost worth
all the misery
framing
these seconds of truth
on all sides

One should have a tape recorder
one should write down
what you're saying
I always think
while you're saying it
and I can't get up

to take out the tape recorder
or find paper and pencil

You really should know this
I keep thinking

But while you are most desperate
and are calling into doubt
all that you've ever done
or will ever do
I realize
that you know

that this is why
you are so
desperate

❖

If I hadn't loved you
so immensely
and if I had not always believed
your words
about this being the last time
definitively and irrevocably
the very last time
that you would drink

then perhaps it would have been easier
to put up with
the times that followed

But you see I always believed
what you said
and loved you
and was convinced that
you really wanted nothing else
but to stop drinking
and never start again

That actually seemed
completely logical
because who would voluntarily
want to go through the hell
that you went through every time
and each time also always seemed
a bit worse
than the previous god-awful time

Sometimes when I despaired
I would ask you
why you hadn't quit
though you had promised for sure
that you would
the last time

Then you answered
that you really
hadn't wanted to stop
deep down
that time or any other time
But, you said, now you wanted to
in a really different
and completely new way
Now you really
never again
wanted to drink
And did I believe you?

Of course I believed you
now that you wanted
really deep deep down
And I loved you, didn't I?

As time went on
I guess I really no longer
believed you
when you assured me
that you'd stop

but I noticed
that I'd been going around
hoping anyway

because each time
I got so terribly
disappointed

Of course one shouldn't
believe or hope
only just love
and be just as
surprised
and grateful
each sober evening
after a sober day

But that's not the way it is
no, it's not like that at all

When I no longer believe
and no longer have the strength to hope
I don't give a damn
whether you're sober
or drunk

I step over you
when you lie there, drunk
I keep the kids at a distance
move my mattress
sleep on the floor in another room

continue
with my work

I live my life
and the kids live theirs

yes, you're bothering us
the hours you're awake
stumbling around
nagging
but you don't concern us
you are no longer
part of our lives

Now you can believe and hope
completely by yourself
we're fed up with
being disappointed
we no longer exist
on your terms

Of all the ways
we've tried
this one seems to be the only one
that really works

Only too bad

it came too late
for me

So it was
my indifference
you needed
while my love apparently
just hurt you

❖

Now I don't have to
be scared anymore
one of them says,
that he'll start
drinking
now that he's started
we can only wait
till he stops

Now I don't have to
come home for dinner
on time today
says another
now that he's drinking
he won't notice
if I skip

dinner today

Bye,
I'm leaving
says a third
takes off
gets home only
after dark
whispers on the sofa
half an hour
now that for once
we've got time
just the two of us

To a fourth one
I read a double-length story
I can well afford to do that
now that he has
passed out
and doesn't sit there
hoping it'll be his turn
sometime

I myself have a nice long
phone conversation
where I don't have to
watch my words

or my inflections
now that there's no one
pricking up his ears
to listen
and try to
misunderstand

Then I stay up
half the night
and write and write and write
now that there's no telling
what I'm up to
and when I don't first
have to go to bed
and wait
until he's sleeping

As long as we are this far
the second day or so
into a drinking bout
when he can still sleep
and while no devils
chase him yet along the walls
all of us are doing
pretty well

❖

In your drunken state
you are omnipotent—
you are prosecutor
you are witness
you are judge
and above all you're the one
who's always sentenced
to guilt and punishment and suffering

So perhaps it's not surprising
that it's hard for you
to avoid taking
the path
where you can be sure
that what you're looking for
always
finds you

❧

If one translates
the binges that render you useless
into women's language
it might be easier to understand
what it's all about—

You imagine

me suffering from nauseous migraines
and lying there greenish pale with a washbowl
next to the bed
(you empty it)

You imagine
me menstruating on the first day
bleeding red and writhing
in pain
(you're stroking my back
talking soothingly and keeping the kids away)

You imagine
that it's impossible for me
to eat, go to the toilet
lie still, be alone
(you change the sheets, mop the floor,
go to the pharmacy in the middle of the night,
give me raw eggs, wake up a child
to sit by me while you're away)

You imagine
that it's best to keep my indisposition
secret, who'd want to employ
a woman who's useless like that
and what will the relatives say
(you speak vaguely

about stomach flu and your nerves
causing trouble)

You imagine
that I really want you to make love to me all this time
even though for twenty years you've known
no good can come of it
when I'm menstruating and won't ever fall asleep
(you pinch your own thigh when I
insist on kissing you
although I reek of drugs and blood and often burp)

You imagine
that many things go with my period
my talking, my nagging, my paranoia
my jealousy, my anger, my suicidal thoughts
(you learn to listen on the surface
but still think your own thoughts,
you never make phone calls from home, you route
your letters
to your job, you hide medications, rope, and knives)

You imagine
that my period lasts seven days or ten or twelve
but that afterward I am serviceable
thirteen whole days
though angry of course and weak

and very gray and pale at first
and then restlessly hectic
when it starts all over again
and thirteen days have run their course
(you take great care not to mention the word menstru-
ation
because I'm very sensitive
and you are warm and mellow and happy that you
have me
you live for me alone
and for life's happy moments)

You finally imagine
—and you think of this often—
that this is the rhythm you and your family
have had to get used to all these years
and that this is the life you have
you and your family
and all the thousands of other families
who have a wife who is useless
at home

◈

"Thousands of male alcoholics
have a woman as a shield
between themselves and uncontrolled drinking

Women do not have this advantage"

(from a Swedish paper)

❖

You're so goddamn perfect
you hiss
so damned flawless
always uptight
and demanding
in control, superior
always accusing me

Yes
I accuse you
of the fact
that you don't see me
as the person I am
but are trying to shape me
according to your needs

into someone who's never wrong
and who therefore can't create disorder
in your authoritarian world

someone who demands that you

know your place
when you yourself don't want to stay put
but don't dare to leave
either

someone who wants to force you
to look yourself in the eyes
and admit
that you don't want to be responsible
for your life

someone who erects barriers
around you
so that you feel you have freedom
above and beyond

someone who'll only raise her eyebrows
when you hurl your invectives
against a world
that's always against you

someone who'll furnish the arguments
you know are right
and that you therefore don't dare
to listen to

someone who blames you

when your guilt overwhelms you
and the only thing that can lighten your burden
for a while
is punishment and suffering

Still a five-year-old, you're asking me
to be the one you never had
fifty years ago—
Your Mother, the Almighty

❖

Upper class alcoholics
are usually able to stay afloat
for many more years
than skid row alcoholics
and the really privileged
upper class alcoholics
don't necessarily ever
need to be known in public
as alcoholics

Upper class alcoholics booze up at home
stock up at the house whatever they need
then take a leave for as long as the binge lasts
with a buffer of secretaries
and children and wives

as protective phone responders

Upper class alcoholics are driven
discreetly by private car
assisted by a faithful old friend
who won't give the secret away
and taken to some private clinic

There, they get a private room with a phone
so they can check on wife
and secretary
and they have access to the ward chief himself
anytime, day or night
to be sure, they can afford the several hundred euros
admission fee
Then they get injections
are sedated for a week
and are finally driven home just as discreetly
with a whole battery of sedatives and vitamins
and tranquilizers
Then they issue a few orders
to their underlings
just to show that they are in complete control
and only need some relaxation

When a few days have passed
they step out into society again

newly showered, massaged
with matching tie and socks
and wearing brand new
underwear
which give them the courage it takes to attack
the laxity that's rampant
among subordinates at work
and at home

❖

Nobody ever
hit me

When I was little
they slapped my wrist and said
No!
After that I never touched
their books on the bookshelf

When I grew older
and wanted to be out
until three o'clock at night
my father said
Headstrong!
Then they invited home all those
whom I would meet between one and three at night

when I was fifteen
And suddenly it wasn't important anymore
to meet them
at night

The time you were chasing me
with the fireplace poker once
years ago
when you were drunk
I wasn't afraid
because the name you shouted
when you lifted the poker
wasn't mine
and soon you calmed down
when I took your hand
and spoke to you
so you heard
that the voice was mine

Nobody ever hit me
and never was I
physically afraid
that someone might
hit me

until you hit me

You have every reason now
to be afraid
of me

❖

In slow motion
you raise the hand
that will strike me

Many thoughts
pass through my mind
before your hand
reaches me

the thought
of all women
in all times
who have known this second
the one before the hand strikes

the fear
that paralyzes
makes me incapable
of getting away
bite kick flee
I can't open my mouth

61

I don't scream
the feeling
of being abandoned
with no turning back
with no options
no strength
no control
not able to do anything

not able to do anything

and finally
the unbelievable
in what's happening to us—
it's inconceivable
it won't happen
it can't happen

you
cannot hit
me

Even before your hand
reaches me
I already know:
this happens to us not
for lack of love

but for love's despair

still
it's hard to comprehend
impossible to forget

❖

Nobody
could have begun life more secure
than I

Nobody
could have been more hopeful
than I

Nobody
could have loved more devotedly
than I

Nobody
could have been more unsuspecting
than I

Nobody nobody
could have been
more fateful

for somebody else
in her all-embracing understanding
in her self-effacing forgiveness

than I

❖

2

___

I love you so immensely
you said
no one has ever been able to love like me
I have built a pyramid of my love
you said
I have placed you on a pedestal
high above the clouds
This is the love story of the century
you said
it will last forever
in eternity it will be admired
you said

I had difficulty sleeping
the first seven hundred and thirty nights
after I'd realized
how immensely you love
your love

❖

We moved in together

not because we
wanted to
but because we
couldn't help it

We don't move
apart
although we want to
because we still can't leave
each other alone

if this is hatred
what then does love look like?

✦

If I could have been
everything you wanted me
to be
the mother
who loves you and forgives you
and understands you and approves of you
who admires you endlessly
and punishes you when you're bad
and makes your decisions
and puts everything right for you
whom you can blame when the world

isn't what you want it to be
who is eternal and everlasting
and who is always there
and stays awake and waits and worries
about you
and no one else but you—

then nothing would have been different
anyway

❖

It probably wasn't at all true
that you fell in love
with my blue striped cotton dress
because I looked so innocent
which I was

or that I was crazy for
your brilliant expressions
and your genius
that hit me
twenty years before it hit the world

but only that
your needs fit mine
—to need and to be needed—

and that both of us
completely lacked
all sense of moderation

Thus, at the starting point
we were
completely equal
if later on things went wrong
the fault was
entirely our own

❖

Early on
I hid my vulnerability
from you

Why would I want to hurt you
by showing you
how much
you had hurt me

that way I managed to prevent
both you and me
from growing

❖

You say
that you love me

My work, however,
you talk about
with contempt and disdain

My monthly salary
you can earn
in one afternoon
while sunning yourself in the yard

My views
you can't find out
because I can't make you hear me
while you are expounding your own

My people
you try to put down
the best you can
as soon as you know
that they are my people

My time
has always existed
for you to use
for your needs

My faithfulness
you claim is important to you
while you yourself of course
have your erotic needs

My despair
over your lack of concern
you see as envy
jealousy

My anguish
during long nights
you soundly sleep through

You who love
can't you sometime
try to tell me what it is you mean
when you say
you love me?

❖

You claim that the whole world
knows my secrets
except you
who never get to hear
anything

Still, it was precisely
so that you would listen
that I placed myself in the market square
with the whole world passing by
and howled out
my secrets

❖

Finally
you used
your love
as an invocation
—so enormous, so all-embracing
so passionate, so unique
you mumbled
swinging the censer
so the world disappeared in a fog

How petty, then
appears
the need for oxygen and fresh air
in comparison with
your tremendous love

❖

You are asking me
what you mean to me
and suddenly it seems
difficult
for me to answer

You were my yearning
to take and to give
one single huge answer to my need
to be needed
You were the one I wanted
to stand equal with
and to have confidence in
the one I wanted to trust
and never let down
whatever happened

You were a challenge so enormous
it seemed inevitable
you were a task
that was too difficult
and therefore necessary
and you were the one I wanted
my children to look like

You were every possibility
and development and future

you were mutual struggle
and the impossible hope
for change

You were fathomless
and I was fathomless
and together we would drown

But along the years
something has happened

Today you are the person
I live with

❖

Dialogue is no longer possible
we have lost the language
we have no dictionary
we can't even read a text
and the rules of grammar we have never learned
—we improvised as we went along

now mouths jabber without sound
arms gesticulate
feet stamp their emphasis
we throw up our arms

we still grasp nothing

But still for some time
we'll keep on trying
in despair and hopelessness

until finally we realize
that we already gave up
very long ago

❖

The more I loved you
the more you doubted
my love
It continuously
had to undergo new and harder tests
And when it always lasted, anyway
and only grew
together with my despair
you finally became
completely beside yourself

Then you hit upon
yet another variation—
to love
even more

than I

You who had written in flaming letters
that you could not love
you who were doomed
to stand apart from life, unloved
and watch
happy people loving
now even you loved
more than I

Nowadays I understand completely
how petty
my love is
for you

❖

There have been times
when you've hurt my feelings
unbearably
only to expect that
the next moment
I'll take you in
as usual
with desire and warmth and devotion

Those times
it has been
a great pleasure for me
not to let myself go
as you assumed I would
Instead, with deliberate precision
and well-tested technique,
I've brought you to a quicker climax
than was your intention
while holding myself back

Not even the smallest fragment
of myself
or my desire or my warmth
or my devotion
do I offer you
if I myself don't feel like it

And all this escapes your attention
as completely as does the fact
that you're hurting my feelings
unbearably

❖

When I'm sleeping with you
I don't have to

listen to you
talk with you
see you

When I'm sleeping with you
my face is so close
to your face
that you can't see me

So I can be myself
at least
when I'm sleeping with you

❖

When you're lying like this
very close to me
still halfway inside me
and I'm breathing your air
and you're breathing mine
and your heartbeat goes through me
then it happens that I wonder
what it was that was so hard
for us to say
what it was that hurt so deeply
was so difficult ever to forget
what it was that made me

no longer love you

no?
longer?
love?
you?

What would happen
if I suddenly stopped
looking for the words
I have sought for twenty years
in vain

If I could suddenly talk
so you could hear
and understand?

What would happen
if suddenly we
dared
to trust each other?

What would happen
if suddenly both of us knew
that there was never anyone else
and that pretending was no longer possible?

What would happen
if neither of us
ever again
lied?

❖

Oh yes, we know each other so well
only too well
for us to remain silent is also
a message
confidence has a thousand ways
to show
that it doesn't exist
treacherous solicitude
stabs you in the back
the mustard gas of suspicion
creeps insidiously along
the ground
filling each crack
with its stench

All the words
we spew out
that should be communication
are camouflage
but neither of us

still manages to hide
anything
from the other

Even honesty
is a weapon
in our hands

We'll never get away
from each other

❖

For me it was easy
to begin with
one would simply love
there was nothing to it
to love
when one had always been surrounded
by love
and when one had learned early on
that love was the biggest
and the happiest
and the best there was

As long as it was love
things went well

But then it became hate
and hate was not allowed
when I was little

What are you supposed to do
about a hatred
that mustn't exist?

You don't use any dirty words
You don't swear
You don't hit
You don't shout
And by no means do you slam the door
You don't make faces
Of course you don't throw
anything
You try to be really friendly
when you're hating

You swallow your hatred
eat it up
hide it
never admit it

For me it wasn't easy
to hate
but the disaster was

not to

❖

I'm sure I can say
(without risking a misunderstanding)
that I love you
you said the day before yesterday

I said nothing the day before yesterday
and not yesterday either
but today I'll say to you
yes I understand you
yes you may say it
yes I'll receive your love
yes I'll give you mine
I love you I love you I love you
without risking a misunderstanding
I dare to love you
I dare to tell you
that I love you
yes!

But somewhere deep inside me I blush
to think that you and I
must resort to parentheses
or wait for two days

when we know
that we love

❖

Carefully you fence in
my life
When did I leave from the office
and when will I get home
and what have I done
that empty half hour
more than my return reasonably
could have taken
even during the rush hour?

Extremely upset
when I've just shaved
my armpits
For whose sake
do I really shave
my armpits?

And besides, what is it
that forces me
to work
and make myself inaccessible
when you can

support me
so I could stay
home and wait for you
all day long?

It might well be
that you think
my freedom can't be
that important
to me
But of course that's only because of
your enormous
love

Why don't I appreciate
your love?

❖

Love and love—
as if love were just one
one single one
a love in a defined and prescribed
and approved form

love between two
who blend and fuse

until neither can be seen
love between two
who turn their backs to the world

love that makes unattainable
and irresponsible
love that is fenced in
and self-sufficient
love that knows its value
only when it excludes everyone else

That love was never mine
that love is dead

❖

For a whole day
we keep squabbling

that I never told you
that you should have helped me
with the kids
and the house
that of course I told you
and told and told and told you
but that you never listened
or understood

or cared to
understand
what I was trying to say

that you never tried to read
my five-hundred-page letter to you
when you were away
because you couldn't see
how it might contain anything
that would be as important
as the fact that you returned
to me

that the only thing you apparently
needed
was my body
not me
not my thoughts
that you never seemed to have had
any use for
by the way

that in case it really only
was the body
then by God
the world is full
of other bodies

that if that's the case
well do as you please
go go go

You hoist the sails
of your old tub
and steer it
seething with anger
into the reeds

I'm chopping kindling
so the splinters
fly
I stick out my tongue
at you

I hate you I hate you I hate you
I can only imagine
how you're cursing
and repudiating me
and my body and my thoughts
out there on the bay

When you return
you sit quietly on the rock, sneer ironically:
"Since I only seem to utter
stupidities

I guess I'd better
just
shut up."

By all means
byallmeans byallmeans

I go in and start
dinner
I always I
of course I
and dinner

I chance to look out
see those sad eyes of yours

I walk around you
on the shore
You idiot, I say
you goddamned stupid idiot
I give you a kiss

you stupid jerk, you say
reluctantly
give me a kiss
seven thousand volts
you rush off and pull in

four pikes
from the sea
give a lecture
on Van Gogh and Georgia O'Keefe
talk talk talk

We talk
talk talk

Well my goodness
how we must
love each other

✦

I feel
that you have failed me
since you've had
no use for me the way I am
but rather have made me into a spirit
who doesn't have character traits
or thoughts or a voice
but who only exists as a casing
around the enormous selfish
masochistic
love
that turns its back to the world

I don't know
how I'll get over
my disappointment

You feel
that I've failed you
that I've felt sympathy
toward your enemies
that I don't want to see
your intentions
that I don't receive
your love
which exists only for me
and never has needed anything else
in the world

You don't know
how you'll get over
your disappointment

So here we stand
showing off
our disappointments
and struggling over
whose are the greatest
and the heaviest

Actually, it is
only now
that we fail

❖

You forced me into a compartment
where I never belonged
you put a mask over my face
which gave you the expressions you needed
as an answer

but they were never my expressions
it was never me behind the mask

While your words were drumming on the mask
I hung it
on the chair opposite you
and went away, singing,
hidden by all your words
that were silently bouncing
against the mild smile
in the chair

When will you notice
that my chair
is empty?

You're a real loner
you trust only yourself
you believe in the brilliance
of the dazzling solo
team play isn't for you

You weigh measure compare
too often underrated
ignored neglected

If someone else
is praised
to you that means
that you're diminished

If someone else
fails
then you have
grown

You never expect well of someone
before you've seen that he's worth it
Everyone else you thoroughly distrust

And most of the time you seem to be right

for the most part apparently it's best
to distrust the people you meet

For the thousandth time
proven wrong
I stand there
and mumble my:

anyway one has to
anyway one has to believe
anyway one has to risk loving

❖

How can I explain
the paradoxical fact
that I need a job
that takes too much of my time
because I have you
who take the rest of the time

As long as I've got the job
I have a context
to belong to
a connection with some of my dearest friends
in a job that seems meaningful
to all of us

As long as I've got the job
I would at least have accomplished something
this day of my life
regardless of what you look like
this particular day

As long as I've got the job
I've got the way there and back
which is my own

Seventeen minutes in the bus
when I have time to read
or turn a poem over in my head
or just mull over something difficult
connected with the place
that's just demanded
all of me
before the next place
that demands all of me
devours me

As long as I've got
my demanding stimulating
numbing job
I've still got someplace
where I can be
without you

so that I'll have the strength
to come home again
to you

❖

A sunny and protected Mediterranean harbor
a repulsive creature who drove her husband to his death
recipient of seven ejaculations in one night, carefully
                              registered and accounted for
a nodding doll who'll deliver infidelity when necessary
a flowerpot to sow brilliance into
a laying hen that hatches beautiful children with the proper
        genes
an ornament that moreover is useful, offers
                              orgasms and admiration
a mirror and an echo, sounding board and background
a fence without which no freedom exists on the other side
a hole and an understanding and a forgiveness
and fourteen or forty-four or four hundred and forty cunts
                              without face or personality

Elevated to a pedestal among the clouds, worshipped and
        threatening,
or else trodden underfoot in utter contempt

But never ever

the person you stand on an equal footing with
every ordinary day

❖

About ten years ago
when in desperation
and with my reserves of young-mother strength
almost depleted
I tried to talk to you
about doing your share
and taking responsibility
for what is
both of ours
you never listened to me
but said
that I was petty
making a fuss
when you were so busy
creating a name
for yourself

What I never understood was
why you insisted
on saying
that you loved me
when you did not even notice

that pretty soon
there would be
nothing left of me to love

Then you made yourself
a name
while I stood there
with reality way up
to my ears

Today
when you have your name
you are also criticized
for your lack of insight
and your ignorance
about reality

And now you come to me
and want me
to tell you
what kind of reality it is
that they are talking about
these new people

❖

How dare you

use people
for what you call
your erotic habits
without investing anything of yourself?

Can't you see
how demeaning it is
even for yourself?

And when you come with your reports
from those kinds of events
and think that the details
will make me want you more
only because you need them
doesn't it occur to you
that I must draw the conclusion
that I, too, am an object
for your erotic habits
the most exploited object
of them all?

Finally, when you
talk about your erotic habits
so deeply ingrained
—you have to have intercourse at least
once a day, all the days you're sober—
doesn't it ever occur to you

that perhaps habits can be transferred
to me too
and that in that case
they're there
also on the days
when you're not sober
and so can't be
used for my habits?

❖

Feel contempt for women, you?
Never in this world
have you heard anything
so absurd

You who've always only appreciated
the women
you've had, well,
dealings with

Felt contempt for them
you really haven't ever
Not even the whores
have you felt contempt for
you say
proudly

Not
even
the whores

you say

❖

While I was away
you went to her in the mornings
to sleep with her
and tell her about yourself
but you wanted to be loyal to me
you said
so you lied to me when I came home
and said that you'd only been chatting a bit
about your job mainly
with her

You only did that because you felt
so loyal toward me
and you didn't want me
to get upset

She and I
used to meet sometimes
and occasionally talk on the phone

and we also talked about you
and how you felt
that you wanted to be loyal
and so you lied

and a pretty long time passed
but then I asked you
why
you think it's better to lie
and you said you loved me so much
that you wanted to be loyal to me
you understand that, you said

I said I really did not understand
why you slept with her at all
if you loved me so much
that you even wanted to be loyal to me
and then you said
oh well one's erotic habits
as you know, you said
and then you asked me how I knew
that you slept with her
and I said that we talked about that too
when we met
or talked on the phone together

and you got extremely upset

That goddamned liar
you said
doesn't she have any feelings at all
about loyalty?

After that you no longer slept with her
although she asked you to
because your erotic habits
didn't need her any longer
couldn't she see

and each time you talked about her
you called her
that goddamned liar
a person
completely lacking
in loyalty

❖

Keep your roses
clear the table
instead

keep your roses
lie a little less
instead

keep your roses
listen to what I say
instead

love me less
respect me more

Keep your roses!

❖

Sometimes
I try to
imagine
what it would be like
if you lived
with Christopher
and your total of
four kids

would you then always
go to the movies just like that
while Christopher
put the kids to bed?

Would it perhaps not
sometimes

occur to you

that Christopher might want to write

or read

or think

by himself

also at times

other than between eleven at night

and six in the morning?

Wouldn't you really

every now and then

be a bit hesitant to demand

that Christopher always drop

everything he's doing

immediately

as you come in through the door

in order to make you some tea

and then admire

what you've been writing

in your quiet study

while he has been busy with

your four children

and the telephone

and cleaned the house

and taken care of dinner

between the moments at the typewriter?

Well I mean, you are
actually
two colleagues
who are doing the same job
and who are judged
by the same criteria

❖

I am a coward
I'm such an incredible coward, you shout
and hit a resounding drumroll
Confess confess confess
that I'm an unbelievable
coward
the most cowardly and wretched
that ever existed

That was brave,
wasn't it, you say
with pleasure
and await
the applause

It comes
of course it comes

So cowardly
so brave
and so honest
that's well done, they say
and give you
a storm of applause

And the more they applaud
the more certain
you can be
that you don't need to catch
what it is
I'm trying to whisper
in your ear:

Darling why
are you so scared
of reality?

&

Your mother
a boyish girl
with narrow hips

most of me
below the waist

all this is clearly
one single
misunderstanding

❖

It was easy for Richard Wright
in the forties, you say
He of course had
all the injustice against blacks
that he could use

And for you right now
there is no problem, you say
You have the women's movement
that you can feed off
until all this injustice against women
is eliminated

It's worse for me
you say and sigh
What will I write about
today?
What can there be to write about
for one who is white
and male
and middle-aged

But just you wait
another twenty years or so
you say triumphantly
When there's no longer
any inequality left—
What are you going to
write about then?

❖

Happy
about people
I get close to

love them to pieces

You warn me—
people are simply not
that wonderful

Doesn't bother me
at all
so much more reason
to love
until I get disappointed

Naïve

you say

That's right
I say

go on loving

❖

Why does my job threaten you
when yours has never threatened me?
Why are my friends rivals to you
when your friends are enjoyable to me?
Why do you listen suspiciously to my intonation
when I talk with my sister on the phone
when your conversations
never seem menacing to me?

Why is your love for me
a threatening worship
that I can never live up to
when my love for you
wanted to be repose
refreshment, togetherness
a platform to stand on
and a trampoline to jump from
when I prepare to tackle

all those important things
I want to be involved in?

Why do you act on me
like a weight that pulls me down
a wedge between myself and my friends
a guilty conscience for me and the children
a sheet of glass between us and the world
a wall of suspicion
that I must climb over
regardless of where I'm going?

What sort of influence do I have on you
when I've made you believe
that all the thoughts I think
are against you?
How can you have gotten the idea
that my road to freedom
goes over your body?
Who gave you the thought
that my life
becomes death for you
and the death of our love?

How loudly must I shout
how silently breathe into your ear
for you to grasp

what I'm trying to tell you—

I don't threaten you
my freedom doesn't hurt you
my love doesn't trample you
it doesn't fight against you

but for us

How slowly do I have to talk
for you to hear—

it is very very urgent now
if we're going to survive

❖

It isn't the great betrayals
that kill love
love expires
from pretty small and almost imperceptible
betrayals

When all these years
without ever noticing
you have me handle
responsibility and garbage

by myself
love has trouble
surviving

The alternatives
as usual
only two

to wake you and shake you
and whip you and force you
to see
and continue to love you

or to let
love
die

❖

Everywhere
I looked for you
who were everywhere
in my world

I tried to change
my world
so it would fit you

looked for you everywhere

but the one I finally found
was myself

     ❖

To me
love can never be
two who huddle together
in a corner
while life surges by

To me
love must always be
many who struggle side by side
—and you and I as well—
right in the middle
right in the midst of life

     ❖

The Chinese write
the word "crisis"
with the sign for "danger"
and the sign for "possibility"

Long have I felt
the danger
that's hanging over you and me
Many times I have wondered why
it hasn't yet
fallen down on us
and crushed us

When you had become
a stranger
walking around next to me
and lying down on top of me
I thought
there was no other way for us
than the way
from zero to minus

I wanted to spare us
that

For a whole day
you sat in the chair
wearing your hat
and your gloves in your hand
ready to go

but you did not go

and I did not
ask you to

Instead, suddenly we talked
with each other
and listened to
what we were saying

Maybe
despite everything, there is
a chance
for us?

❖

Every day
I lived with you
I did so
because I wanted to

Every time
that it was you
and no one else for me
it was because it was you
I wanted

Always

when I came back to you
it was because it was
together with you
and no one else
that I wanted to be

Only
when you dare to believe
that this day
and all other days
are a free choice for me
—you or not you—

can you and I go on
living
together

3

—

My mother's grandmother
used to write secretly during the night
at her white Empire desk
During the day she was the cabinet minister's wife
until the cabinet minister died
then she published the books she had written

but her diary
could never be published
it was too indiscreet
and at seventeen I wasn't allowed to read it

I read it of course
but thought it was boring
I didn't understand what she was all about

Why did she not get a divorce
from that domestic tyrant?

A couple of times a year
my mother got her attacks
her forehead seemed taut and she looked past us

with a strangely shrill and monotonous voice
she avoided our
anxious and irritated questions

A few days later
when someone could get her to speak
she would always say the same thing—
that she didn't have a desk
where she could sit and write

Father was sitting with tears in his eyes
in his study
arranging the pencils in order of length
But she knows we don't have the space
for yet another desk he said
now that you're all growing and need your own nooks

When yet another day had passed
Mother came out with her usual forehead
and said in her usual voice
that Father was so kind
and that she had been silly again
and she hugged us all

We heaved a sigh of relief
and everything continued
and everyone could go on doing their homework

at their respective desks
and, occasionally, take a break to talk
to Mother
sitting there in the easy chair of the living room
which opened up to other rooms, was telephone room,
     coffee room, and parlor

My mother held her typewriter
in her lap
when she wrote

❖

I was sitting next to my mother
holding her hand
when her light blue eyes grew dim

That moment I promised her
that I would never
say what she had said:
I haven't had the chance

What I will say
if I have to, is:

I didn't take the chance

❖

The older I get
the more I love
my mother
the more I miss her
the better I understand her
the more of her characteristics
I find to my surprise
in myself

I would like to write
about my mother
and about my mother's grandmother
and my maternal grandmother
and my paternal grandmother
and my father's grandmother

I would like to write
about the mothers
I would like to write
about Fredrika
I would like to write
about all of them
who are dead
and whom I love and miss

and who were called Margit
Julia
Emma Ester
and Aurora Concordia

and who were married to Runeberg
and Gösta and Alfred
and Uno and Adam Edvin and Gustaf Adolf

I would like to write
about their legacy
and what they saw and knew and felt
all they managed
to put up with
all they believed in and hoped for
and loved

❖

They had been married nineteen years
and every Wednesday night
she packed his black bag
for that's when he went to the other one
and when he returned home again
on Saturday
she unpacked his black bag
and put his clothes to soak

but one night
she ran out into the forest
and thought that she would die

When the children found her in the morning
she said that she wouldn't pack the bag
never ever again
will she pack his bag
and she'll never see him again

He cried a bit
because he would gladly have continued
to live with her
from Saturday to Wednesday each week
and then of course
there was that laundry

that winter she thought
she would die

When the delivery guy from the florist came
in the spring
with twenty red roses on their anniversary
and a card that said
THANK YOU FOR TWENTY HAPPY YEARS
she said nothing
but took the roses

and tore every leaf off them
and smashed
the stems
and slowly and resolutely
she dumped everything on the delivery guy

❖

Sister
you say you're a compulsive eater
and emotionally undernourished
and your equilibrium a refusal to pry deep
sister
I eat compulsively
to be able to stand my great common sense
and my big feelings sit forlornly beside me
all my feelings
and I
through the nights on my sofa

What is happening to us?
Did you know her, who shot herself last Tuesday
at dawn
after a white night?
All her acquaintances
were surprised

and upset of course
but most of all surprised
She who was so strong
She who was always happy and outgoing
active in the community
and the whole big family

She seemed to have gotten over that thing with her
        husband
that he left her
that she was left alone in a house that was too big
an impressive house, nine rooms
the finances apparently were a bit of a problem
the house was hard to sell
but she had gotten over it everyone says
and seemed strong and happy like before
and had started working full time
seemed to be in fine shape last fall
say people who knew her

I never even met her
and I don't know anything about her last night
or the spring or the summer and fall
or all the white nights of this past winter
when it snows and snows
and snows
throughout the nights

but her dawn
sister
both you and I recognize

❖

I can forgive her everything
That her behind is too fat
and her chin too pointed
that she insists on working
even when it's unnecessary, well
suppose it can't be helped
and she'll probably tire
That she doesn't listen the way I'd like her to
that she doesn't applaud every time
and admire as she should, I
understand of course that genius can get
tiring, it's hard
to vary your words of praise
I understand that
and—most of the time—I forgive her

But I'll never forgive her
that she gave herself to me
but remained
herself

❖

Just like those who forgive
seven times
and seventy times seven
so do I

There's only one time
that I cannot forgive:
the first time
the first betrayal

After that time
I'll forgive no matter how many betrayals
I'm indifferent to them
they don't concern me
and I'm happy to say
that I've forgotten them and forgiven

but that first betrayal
was one too many
to forgive

❖

What they cannot
forgive

is that she changed objects
for her passion
but kept the passion

and so he was left out again
the little Strindberg

❖

When I wake up in the morning
a poem sits in my head
singing

I'll write it down right away
so I won't forget it
it's got such a good rhythm
that poem

I'll just
fix some tea and eggs and cereal
set the table
eat with the others
clear the table and clean up
put things back in the fridge
find something
to occupy big and small ones
when it rains

and then make myself a pot of coffee
I can enjoy
while I'm sitting
at the typewriter

how was it again that it started
that poem?

Someone gets angry
because I said
that I'm the one who runs
everything in this house
another one because I hadn't
covered the ping-pong table
and then it rained
last night
one comes and wants to
talk
What is it that you're writing
all the time?

two start a fight
one is crying
needs lots of hugs to feel better
then three sit and draw pictures
and talk constantly about
what they're drawing

What do lilacs look like?
Do they go straight out
on both sides
and at the top too
those lilacs?

then they sing
three different songs
at the same time

That's when I go outside to pick
a branch of lilacs in the rain
and hope that perhaps it
might find the rhythm
for my poem

Lilacs do grow straight out
at the top
but those flowers could not care less
about my
poems

❖

Isn't it lucky though
you say
that your migraine

is not of the same difficult kind
as grandmother's

Grandmother
had to stay in bed for several days
in her room with curtains pulled
and the maid and the cook and the nanny
had to do everything themselves
without grandmother's help
and everybody tiptoed around
and nobody could turn the pages
of the newspaper
because they rustled
and hurt grandmother's head

How lucky
you say
that you can get over
your migraine with medicine
you who have so many kids
to take care of

❖

I won't allow
my work to take time
away from my family

this I promised myself
when I escaped from suburbia
the last second

That's why I smooth out the lines
on my forehead
when I go through the doorway
in the evening
the smoother my forehead
the more tired I am

That's why I often smile
when I'm home
the more I smile
the bigger the troubles I've got
to deal with on the job

That's why I read stories
with a mild voice
and sit for hours on bedsides
and listen to ABBA
The more I'm predicting scores
of ice hockey matches
the more absorbed I am
in my own problems

That's why I completely agree

with all your theories of art
and all your denunciations of the Russian Premier

I always agree completely
am extra ready
for acrobatic sex
the more intensely I long to
sit down at the typewriter

I almost totally manage
to hide from my family
that I too have
a life of my own
to live

❖

Without those
who share my working days
it would be hard for me
to work
impossible
to live

❖

In a world of

grayish white
grayish blue
grayish brown
a hostile world
a rejecting world
that at best could be said to be
on guard

were her brown eyes

Together
we bought
two yellow cups with orange patterns
a tentative beginning
in order to conquer
the grayish white chill in our office

Sometimes
things went well
then we got ourselves
—wild with joy—
the yellow curtains
in a room that we made
green as seawater

Sometimes everything stood still
or went

backwards
Then we shed salty tears together
into the yellow cups

We became more numerous
pretty soon we were many who worked together
We created a soft room
in beige and brown
and bought a dozen
orange cups
We invited anyone
who dropped in
to share our hopes
and our disappointments
Gradually we were many supporting each other

But always when the going was really tough
it still was she and I
only she and I

the yellow cups
and her brown eyes

❖

I'm sitting here waiting
for you to go

so that I can start to think
all the time conscious
that you haven't gone yet
that there's still a chance that you'll
change your mind
anytime
and not go at all
or that you'll come in once more
interrupting me
so that everything I've just thought out
and everything that feels as if it
almost could be
thought about
simply disappears
and is gone

You fool
I tell myself
You can't just sit there
and wait
all your life long
It'll never be your turn
if you just keep waiting

so I put a sheet of paper
into the typewriter
Oh well, let's see

That's when you come in
and tell me that now you're going
and tell me what you're going to do
and what you're thinking
about this day
and this life
and chat a bit
in a friendly way
with my silent neck

You fool
I tell myself
He is just being friendly
maybe he has no way of knowing
that you are sitting there wanting to think
and besides you have already
stopped thinking
in any case
so you might just as well
be a bit friendly in return

Oh well
so I'm being friendly in return

but then you leave
because all this time of course
you've been on your way

And here I sit waiting
to be able to think
about something other
than the fact that you left

Oh well
well

❖

Though I'm aware
that people die
from lack of other people

I almost can't stand
shouts and voices
laughter and talk demands and love
closeness crowding
everything that spills over me
every second

Shrewd and cunning
revolutionary and bold
I then struggle for my right
to the hours of solitude on the sofa
in the middle of the night

❖

It's only much later
that I realize
how important it would have been
to have kept my own name
a name that is mine
since I frivolously exchanged it
for another's

It's only when I'm witnessing
your exquisite method
of depriving objectionable persons
of their names
and distorting them
that I realize what it's all about

"That Laurén-Saurén"
of the Marxist Leif Salmén
and "that Bergbom
is someone you know I suppose"
of the feminist Maria Bergom-Larsson

Only then I see
how you deprive people
of their intrinsic value
and depreciate them, render them harmless

when you strip them
of their name

MÄRTA ELEONORA CAVONIUS

❖

They think it's courage
that makes me
choose the struggle

compulsion it is
to try to change things

They think it's my will to fight
that makes me
choose the challenge

dread it is
that everything will just continue

They think I'm thick-skinned
because I struggle and challenge

cry is what I do

can't help doing what I'm doing

❖

It's time
for us
to scrap
our guilty conscience, sisters

this society
lives
off our guilty conscience

no need at all
to bother about
oppressing us
as long as we
oppress ourselves

Enough of this now

Now it is time
to scrap
our guilty conscience, sisters

Now it's up
to us to
allow ourselves

the disappointment
the anger
the rage
the hate

When we're done hating
we'll get up
and go

❖

What's done
while our hands are still shaking
in indignation
in anger
is perhaps not the greatest
or eternal

it's too rushed
to choose its words
it's too mighty
to accept boundaries
it's been waiting
too long
to be contained

We can't afford

to leave it undone

❖

Slowly
but step by step
we are making
progress

we've got to believe that

❖

When the ground is heaving
I take small small steps
almost entirely
imperceptible ones
maybe then I can
maintain my balance

When the seconds
pile up
and then come rushing over me
all at once
I am very severe with them
I have to be

One by one, one by one
they get permission to pass me
and the endless hours
until morning

When pages and passages
and sentences
seem impenetrable
I take the words
one after the other
and hold them up to the light
so they become
transparent

Then I gather up
the miniscule remains
of my courage
and whisper quietly
but only to those
with their ear close to the ground
who are slowly inching forward
like me

Stefan Bremer

Märta Tikkanen is a Finnish-Swedish journalist, writer, and teacher. Much of her writing deals critically with gender roles and the shackles that bind women, as well as women's liberation and the desire for self-realization. She became a central figure in the Nordic women's movement with her novel *Manrape* (1978), which was adapted into a 1978 film directed by Jörn Donner. She is the recipient of several awards for her work, including the Nordic Women's Alternative Literature Prize, Finland's State Prize for the Dissemination of Knowledge, the Swedish De Nios Grand Prize, the Swedish Academy's Finland Prize, and Finland's State Literary Prize. Her work has been translated into more than twenty languages. She lives in Helsinki, Finland.

Stina Katchadourian is an author and a translator living in Stanford, California. Her most recent book is *The Lapp King's Daughter*, a World War II memoir from her native Finland based on her parents' correspondence and her own personal memories. Her translations have won her the Pushcart Prize, the Södergran Prize, and the Translation Prize of the American-Scandinavian Foundation.

Thank you all
for your support.
We do this for you,
and could not do
it without you.

 DEEP
VELLUM

PARTNERS

pixel ||| texel

RAYMOND JAMES®

FORTHCOMING FROM DEEP VELLUM

AMANG · *Raised by Wolves*
translated by Steve Bradbury · TAIWAN

MARIO BELLATIN · *Mrs. Murakami's Garden*
translated by Heather Cleary · MEXICO

MAGDA CARNECI · *FEM*
translated by Sean Cotter · ROMANIA

MIRCEA CĂRTĂRESCU · *Solenoid*
translated by Sean Cotter · ROMANIA

MATHILDE CLARK · *Lone Star*
translated by Martin Aitken · DENMARK

PETER DIMOCK · *Daybook from Sheep Meadow* · USA

LEYLÂ ERBIL · *A Strange Woman*
translated by Nermin Menemencioğlu · TURKEY

FERNANDA GARCIA LAU · *Out of the Cage*
translated by Will Vanderhyden · ARGENTINA

ANNE GARRÉTA · *In/concrete*
translated by Emma Ramadan · FRANCE

GOETHE · *Faust*
translated by Zsuzsanna Ozsváth and Frederick Turner · GERMANY

PERGENTINO JOSÉ · *Red Ants: Stories*
translated by Tom Bunstead and the author · MEXICO

JUNG YOUNG MOON · *Arriving in a Thick Fog*
translated by Mah Eunji and Jeffrey Karvonen · SOUTH KOREA

FOWZIA KARIMI · *Above Us the Milky Way: An Illuminated Alphabet* · USA

TAISIA KITAISKAIA · *The Nightgown & Other Poems* · USA

DMITRY LIPSKEROV · *The Tool and the Butterflies*
translated by Reilly Costigan-Humes & Isaac Stackhouse Wheeler · RUSSIA

GORAN PETROVIĆ · *At the Lucky Hand, aka The Sixty-Nine Drawers*
translated by Peter Agnone · SERBIA

C.F. RAMUZ · *Jean-Luc Persecuted*
translated by Olivia Baes · SWITZERLAND

ETHAN RUTHERFORD · *Farthest South & Other Stories* · USA

TATIANA RYCKMAN · *The Ancestry of Objects* · USA

MIKE SOTO · *A Grave Is Given Supper: Poems* · USA

MUSTAFA STITOU · *Two Half Faces*
translated by David Colmer · NETHERLANDS